GHOSTBUSTERS™

VOLUME ONE: THE MAN FROM THE MIRROR, PART 2

WRITTEN BY **ERIK BURNHAM** • ART BY **DAN SCHOENING**

COLORS BY **LUIS ANTONIO DELGADO**

LETTERS BY **SHAWN LEE** AND **NEIL UYETAKE**

EDITS BY **TOM WALTZ** • ASSOCIATE EDITS BY **BOBBY CURNOW**

 Spotlight

ABDOPUBLISHING.COM

Reinforced library bound edition published in 2017 by Spotlight, a division of ABDO PO Box 398166, Minneapolis, Minnesota 55439. Spotlight produces high-quality reinforced library bound editions for schools and libraries.
Published by agreement with IDW.

Printed in the United States of America, North Mankato, Minnesota.
042016
092016

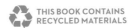

THIS BOOK CONTAINS RECYCLED MATERIALS

IDW

GHOSTBUSTERS, VOLUME 1: THE MAN FROM THE MIRROR. MARCH 2012. FIRST PRINTING.

Originally published as GHOSTBUSTERS Issues #1–4.

LIBRARY OF CONGRESS CATALOGING-IN-PUBLICATION DATA

Names: Burnham, Eric, author. | Schoening, Dan, illustrator.
Title: Ghostbusters. Volume 1, The man from the mirror / writer: Erik Burnham ; art: Dan Schoening ; colors: Luis Antonio Delgado.
Other titles: Man from the mirror
Description: Reinforced library bound edition. | Minneapolis, Minnesota : Spotlight, 2017.
Identifiers: LCCN 2015050198| ISBN 9781614794851 (part 1) | ISBN 9781614794868 (part 2) | ISBN 9781614794875 (part 3) | ISBN 9781614794882 (part 4)
Subjects: LCSH: Graphic novels. | CYAC: Graphic novels.
Classification: LCC PZ7.7.B88 Gho 2016 | DDC 741.5/973--dc23
LC record available at https://lccn.loc.gov/2015050198

ABDO
Spotlight

A Division of ABDO
abdopublishing.com

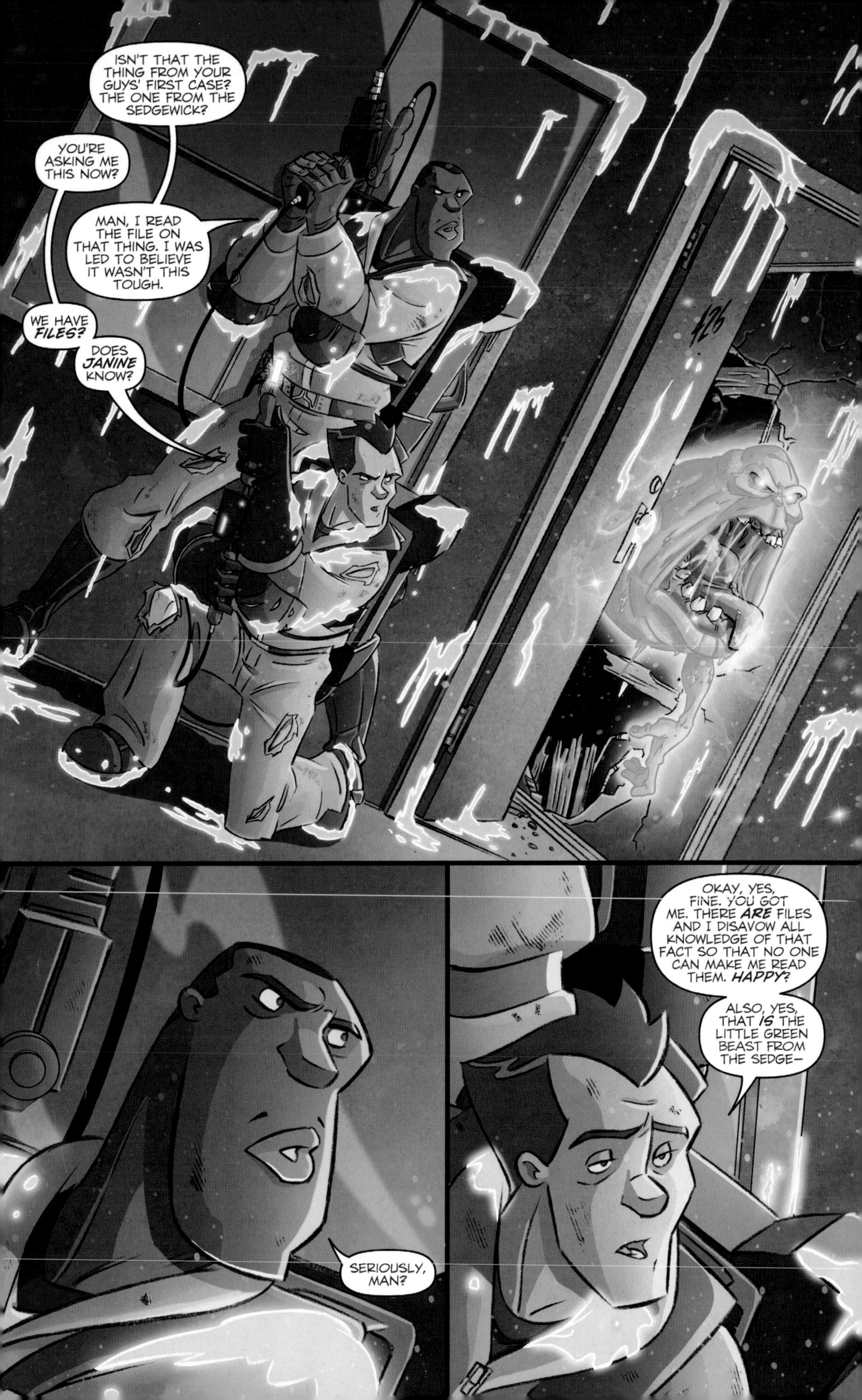

ISN'T THAT THE THING FROM YOUR GUYS' FIRST CASE? THE ONE FROM THE SEDGEWICK?
YOU'RE ASKING ME THIS NOW?
MAN, I READ THE FILE ON THAT THING. I WAS LED TO BELIEVE IT WASN'T THIS TOUGH.
WE HAVE *FILES*?
DOES *JANINE* KNOW?
SERIOUSLY, MAN?
OKAY, YES, FINE. YOU GOT ME. THERE *ARE* FILES AND I DISAVOW ALL KNOWLEDGE OF THAT FACT SO THAT NO ONE CAN MAKE ME READ THEM. *HAPPY?*
ALSO, YES, THAT *IS* THE LITTLE GREEN BEAST FROM THE SEDGE–

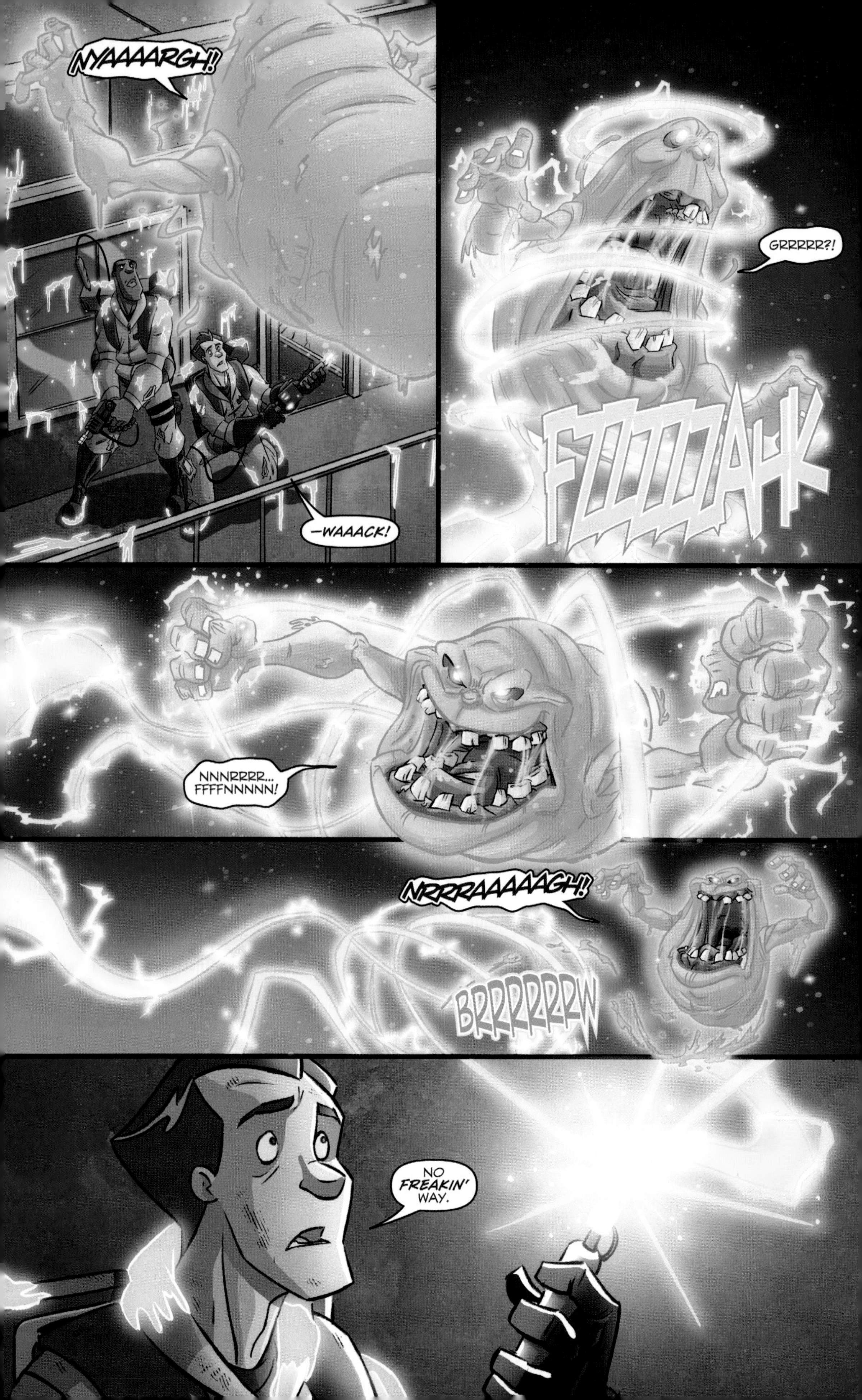
NYAAAARGH!
—WAAACK!
GRRRRR?!
FZZZZZAHK
NNNRRRR... FFFFNNNNN!
NRRRAAAAAGH!
BRRRRRRRW
NO FREAKIN' WAY.

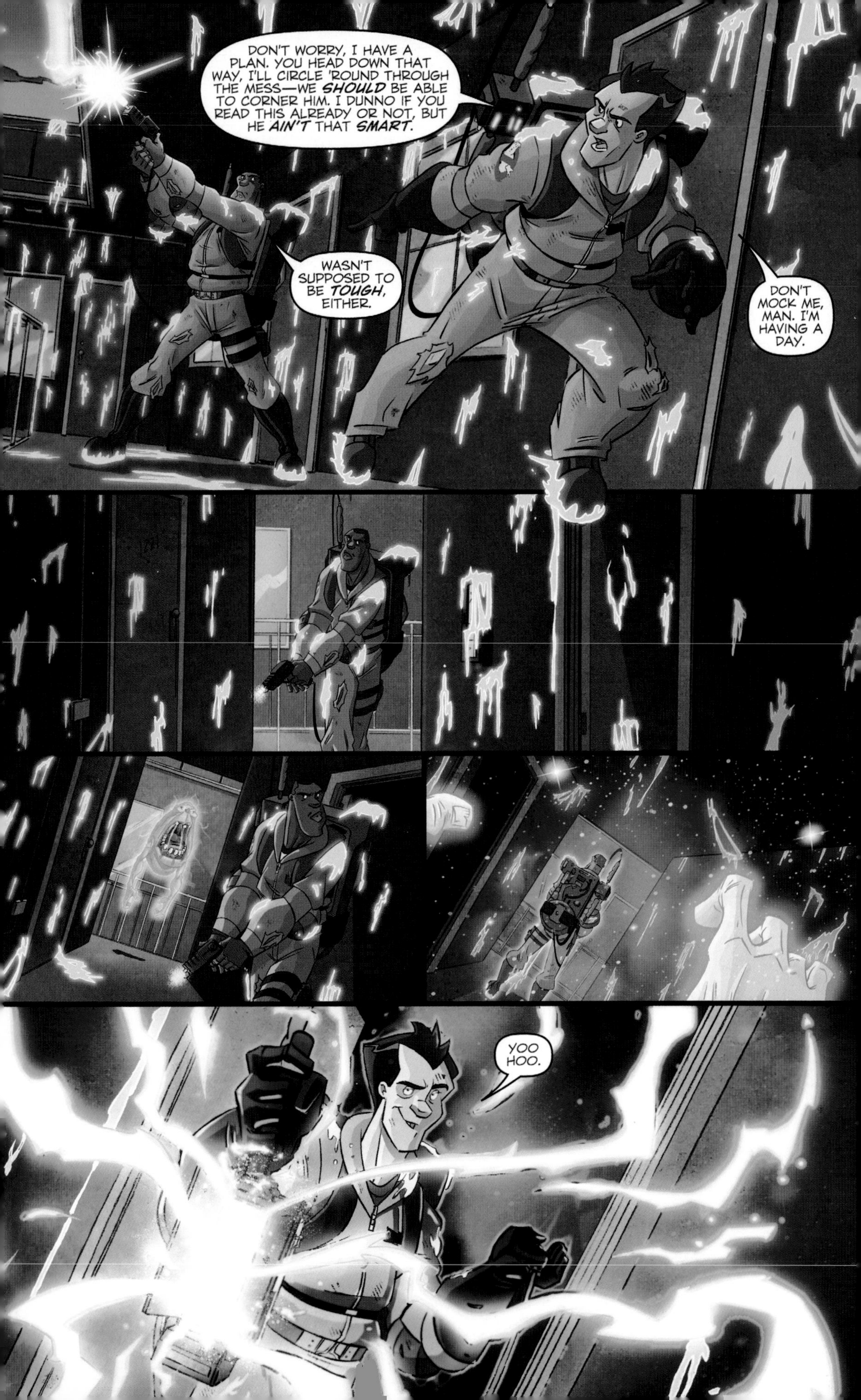
DON'T WORRY, I HAVE A PLAN. YOU HEAD DOWN THAT WAY, I'LL CIRCLE 'ROUND THROUGH THE MESS—WE **SHOULD** BE ABLE TO CORNER HIM. I DUNNO IF YOU READ THIS ALREADY OR NOT, BUT HE **AIN'T** THAT **SMART**.
WASN'T SUPPOSED TO BE **TOUGH**, EITHER.
DON'T MOCK ME, MAN. I'M HAVING A DAY.
YOO HOO.

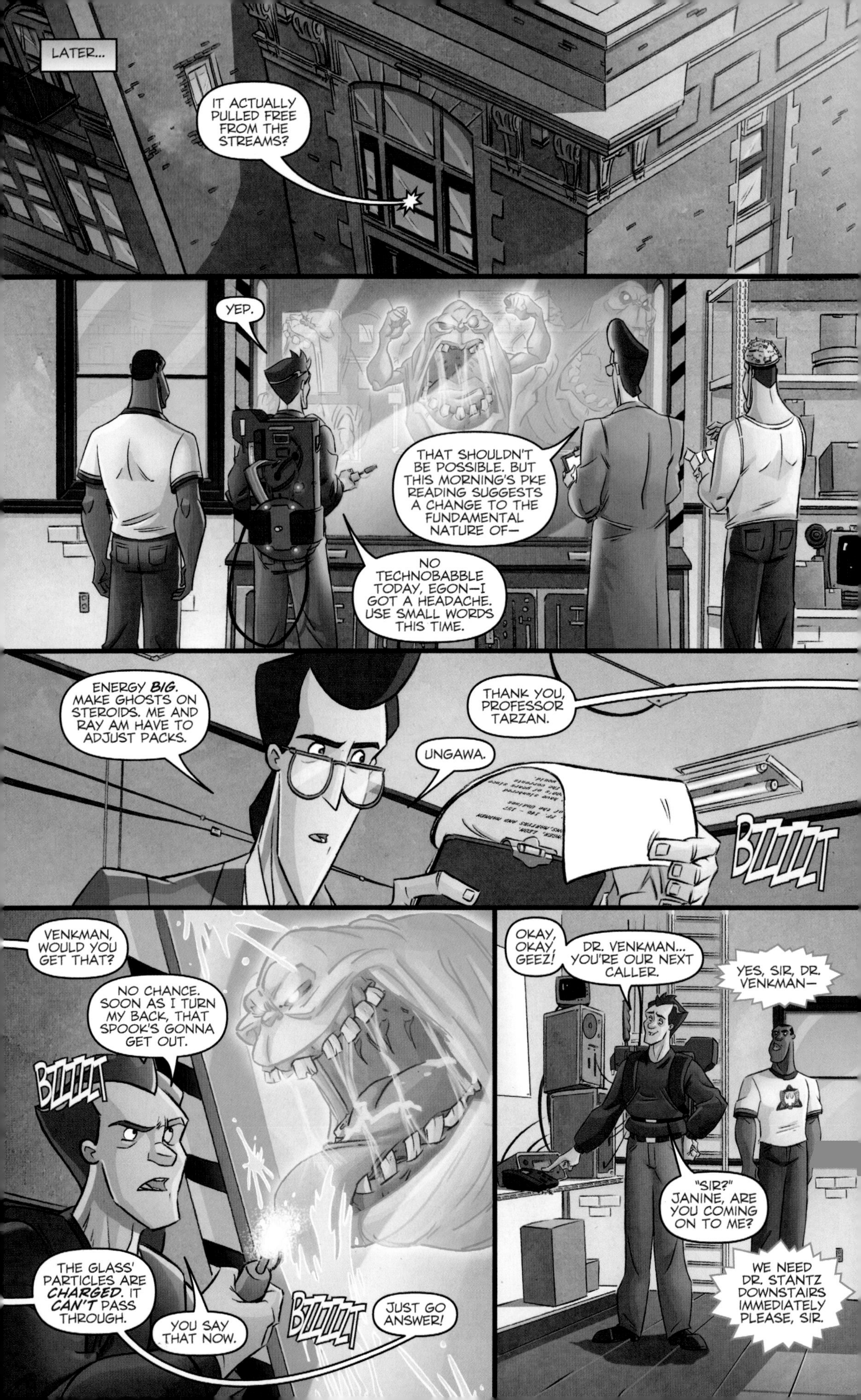
LATER...
IT ACTUALLY PULLED FREE FROM THE STREAMS?
YEP.
THAT SHOULDN'T BE POSSIBLE. BUT THIS MORNING'S PKE READING SUGGESTS A CHANGE TO THE FUNDAMENTAL NATURE OF—
NO TECHNOBABBLE TODAY, EGON—I GOT A HEADACHE. USE SMALL WORDS THIS TIME.
ENERGY BIG. MAKE GHOSTS ON STEROIDS. ME AND RAY AM HAVE TO ADJUST PACKS.
THANK YOU, PROFESSOR TARZAN.
UNGAWA.
BZZZZT
VENKMAN, WOULD YOU GET THAT?
NO CHANCE. SOON AS I TURN MY BACK, THAT SPOOK'S GONNA GET OUT.
BZZZZT
THE GLASS' PARTICLES ARE CHARGED. IT CAN'T PASS THROUGH.
YOU SAY THAT NOW.
BZZZZT
JUST GO ANSWER!
OKAY, OKAY, GEEZ!
DR. VENKMAN... YOU'RE OUR NEXT CALLER.
YES, SIR, DR. VENKMAN—
"SIR?" JANINE, ARE YOU COMING ON TO ME?
WE NEED DR. STANTZ DOWNSTAIRS IMMEDIATELY PLEASE, SIR.

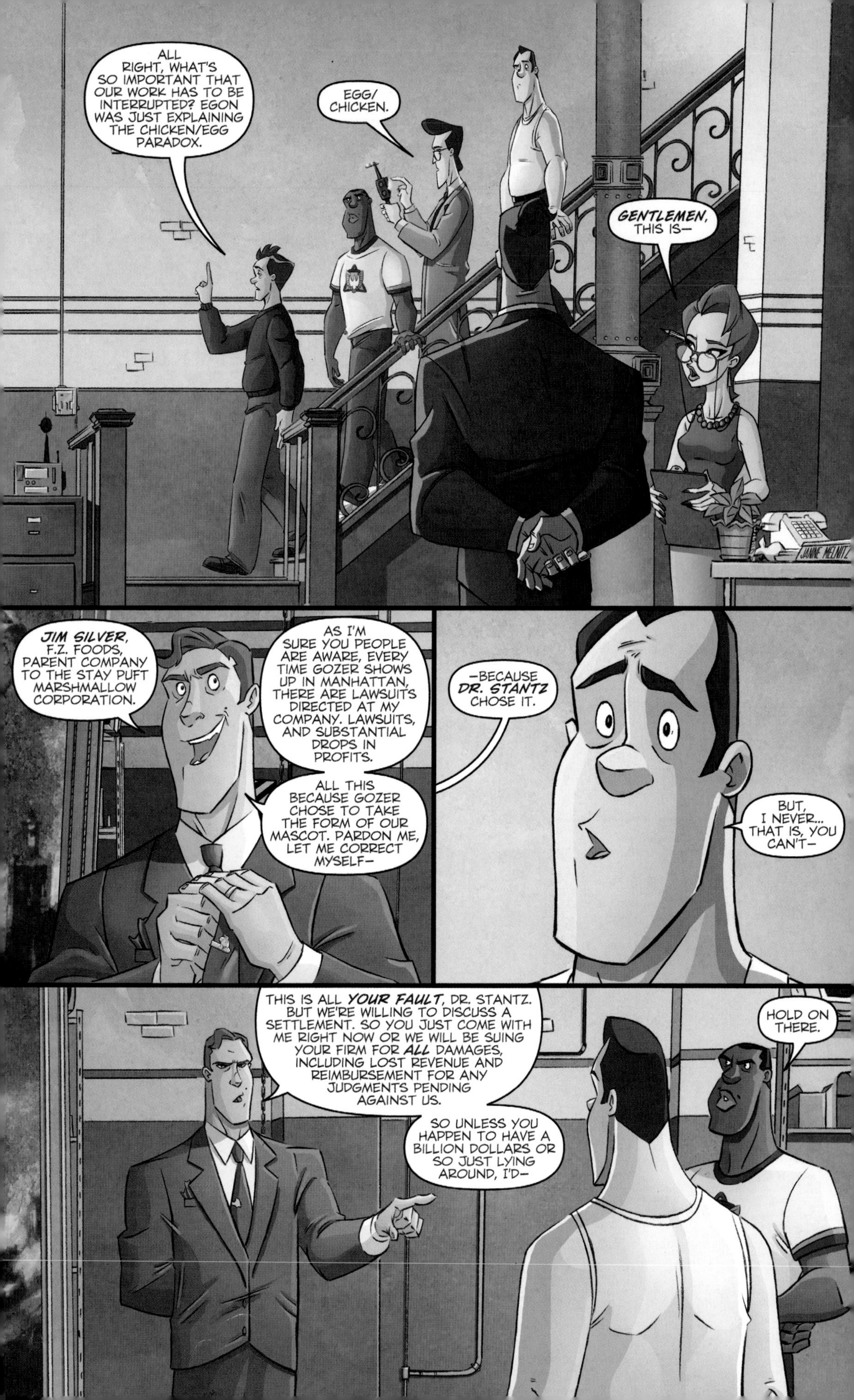
ALL RIGHT, WHAT'S SO IMPORTANT THAT OUR WORK HAS TO BE INTERRUPTED? EGON WAS JUST EXPLAINING THE CHICKEN/EGG PARADOX.
EGG/ CHICKEN.
GENTLEMEN, THIS IS—
JANINE MELNITZ
JIM SILVER, F.Z. FOODS, PARENT COMPANY TO THE STAY PUFT MARSHMALLOW CORPORATION.
AS I'M SURE YOU PEOPLE ARE AWARE, EVERY TIME GOZER SHOWS UP IN MANHATTAN, THERE ARE LAWSUITS DIRECTED AT MY COMPANY. LAWSUITS, AND SUBSTANTIAL DROPS IN PROFITS.
ALL THIS BECAUSE GOZER CHOSE TO TAKE THE FORM OF OUR MASCOT. PARDON ME, LET ME CORRECT MYSELF—
—BECAUSE DR. STANTZ CHOSE IT.
BUT, I NEVER... THAT IS, YOU CAN'T—
THIS IS ALL YOUR FAULT, DR. STANTZ. BUT WE'RE WILLING TO DISCUSS A SETTLEMENT. SO YOU JUST COME WITH ME RIGHT NOW OR WE WILL BE SUING YOUR FIRM FOR ALL DAMAGES, INCLUDING LOST REVENUE AND REIMBURSEMENT FOR ANY JUDGMENTS PENDING AGAINST US.
SO UNLESS YOU HAPPEN TO HAVE A BILLION DOLLARS OR SO JUST LYING AROUND, I'D—
HOLD ON THERE.

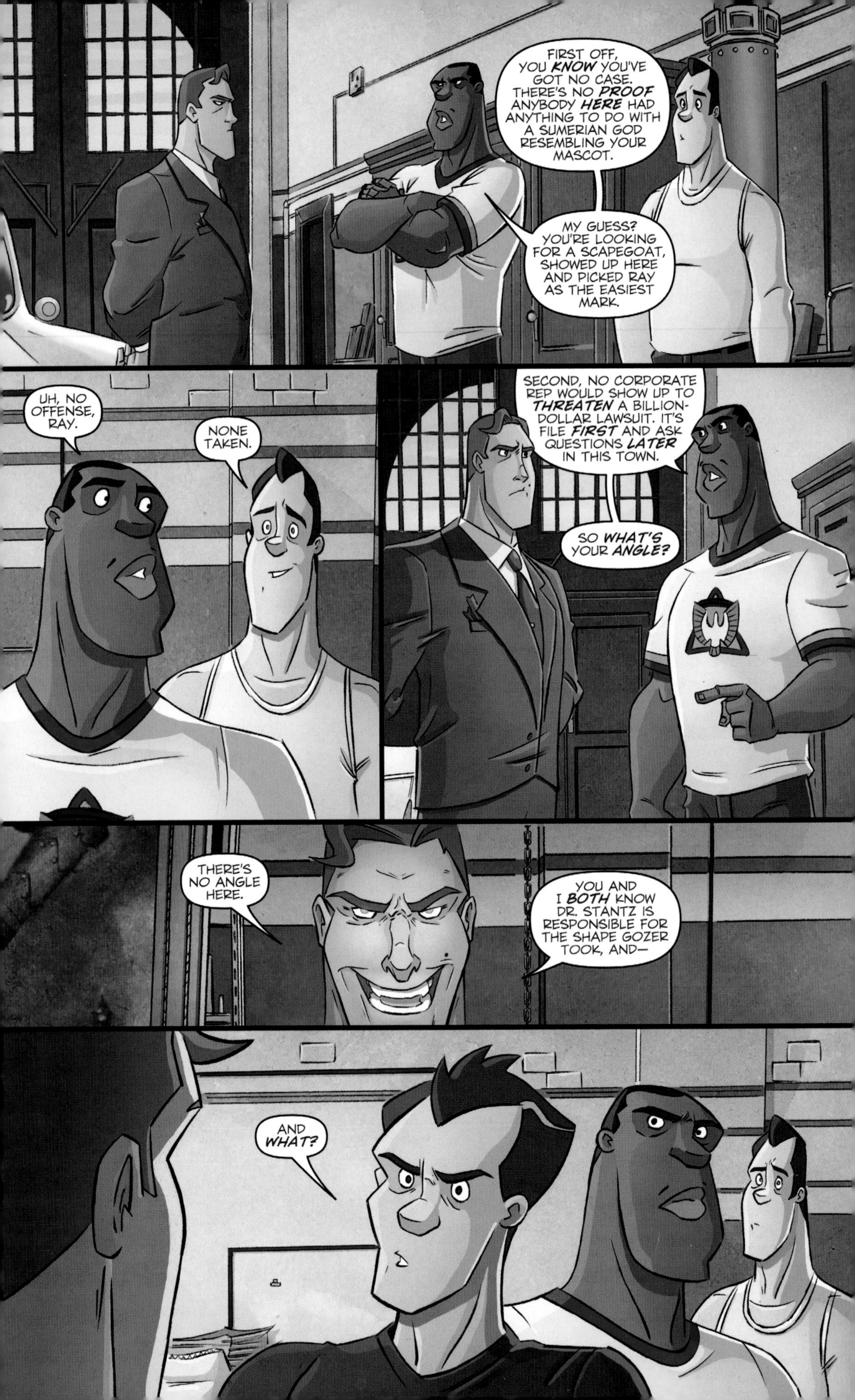
FIRST OFF, YOU KNOW YOU'VE GOT NO CASE. THERE'S NO PROOF ANYBODY HERE HAD ANYTHING TO DO WITH A SUMERIAN GOD RESEMBLING YOUR MASCOT.
MY GUESS? YOU'RE LOOKING FOR A SCAPEGOAT, SHOWED UP HERE AND PICKED RAY AS THE EASIEST MARK.
UH, NO OFFENSE, RAY.
NONE TAKEN.
SECOND, NO CORPORATE REP WOULD SHOW UP TO THREATEN A BILLION-DOLLAR LAWSUIT. IT'S FILE FIRST AND ASK QUESTIONS LATER IN THIS TOWN.
SO WHAT'S YOUR ANGLE?
THERE'S NO ANGLE HERE.
YOU AND I BOTH KNOW DR. STANTZ IS RESPONSIBLE FOR THE SHAPE GOZER TOOK, AND—
AND WHAT?

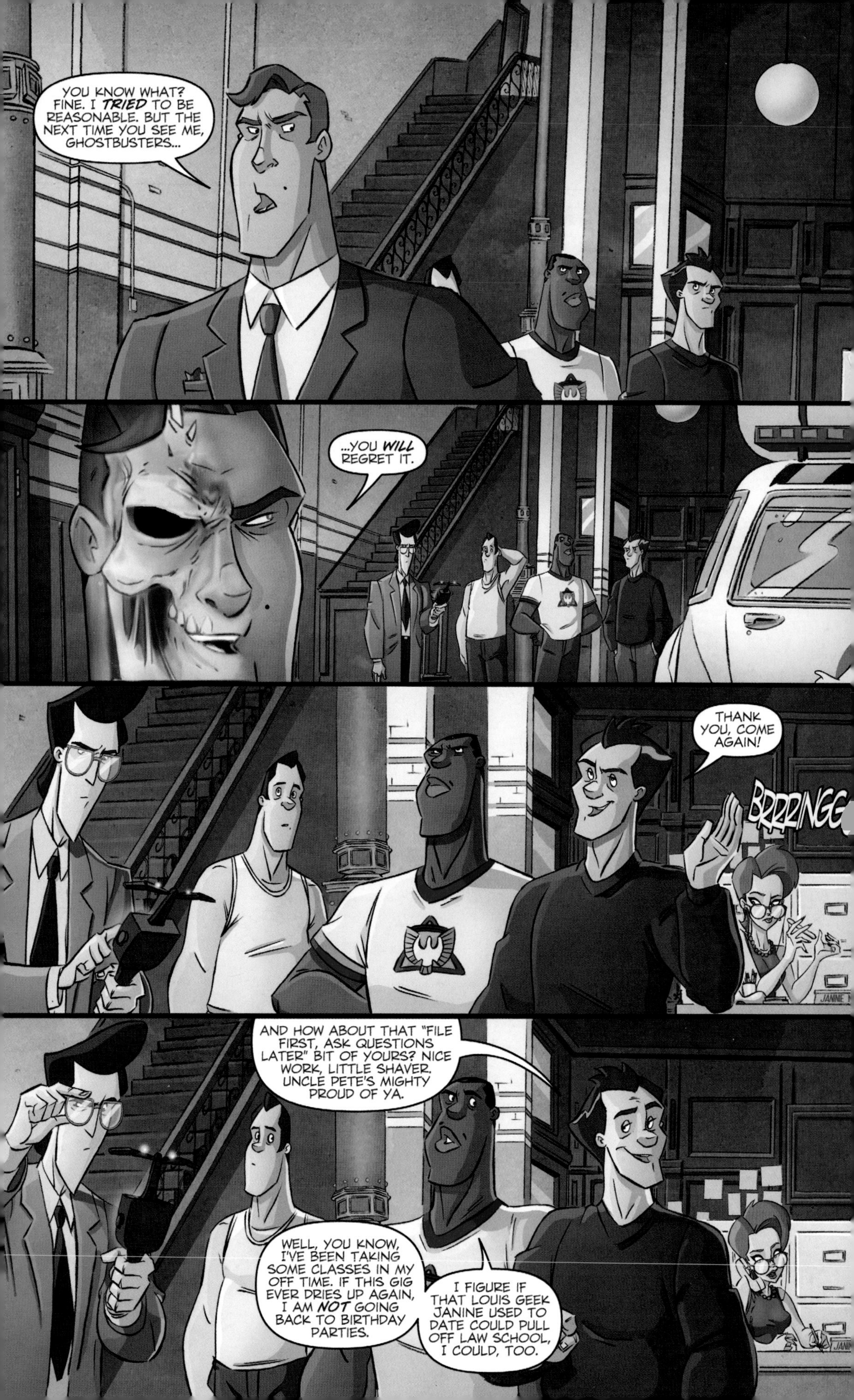
YOU KNOW WHAT? FINE. I TRIED TO BE REASONABLE. BUT THE NEXT TIME YOU SEE ME, GHOSTBUSTERS...
...YOU WILL REGRET IT.
THANK YOU, COME AGAIN!
BRRRINGG
AND HOW ABOUT THAT "FILE FIRST, ASK QUESTIONS LATER" BIT OF YOURS? NICE WORK, LITTLE SHAVER. UNCLE PETE'S MIGHTY PROUD OF YA.
WELL, YOU KNOW, I'VE BEEN TAKING SOME CLASSES IN MY OFF TIME. IF THIS GIG EVER DRIES UP AGAIN, I AM NOT GOING BACK TO BIRTHDAY PARTIES.
I FIGURE IF THAT LOUIS GEEK JANINE USED TO DATE COULD PULL OFF LAW SCHOOL, I COULD, TOO.

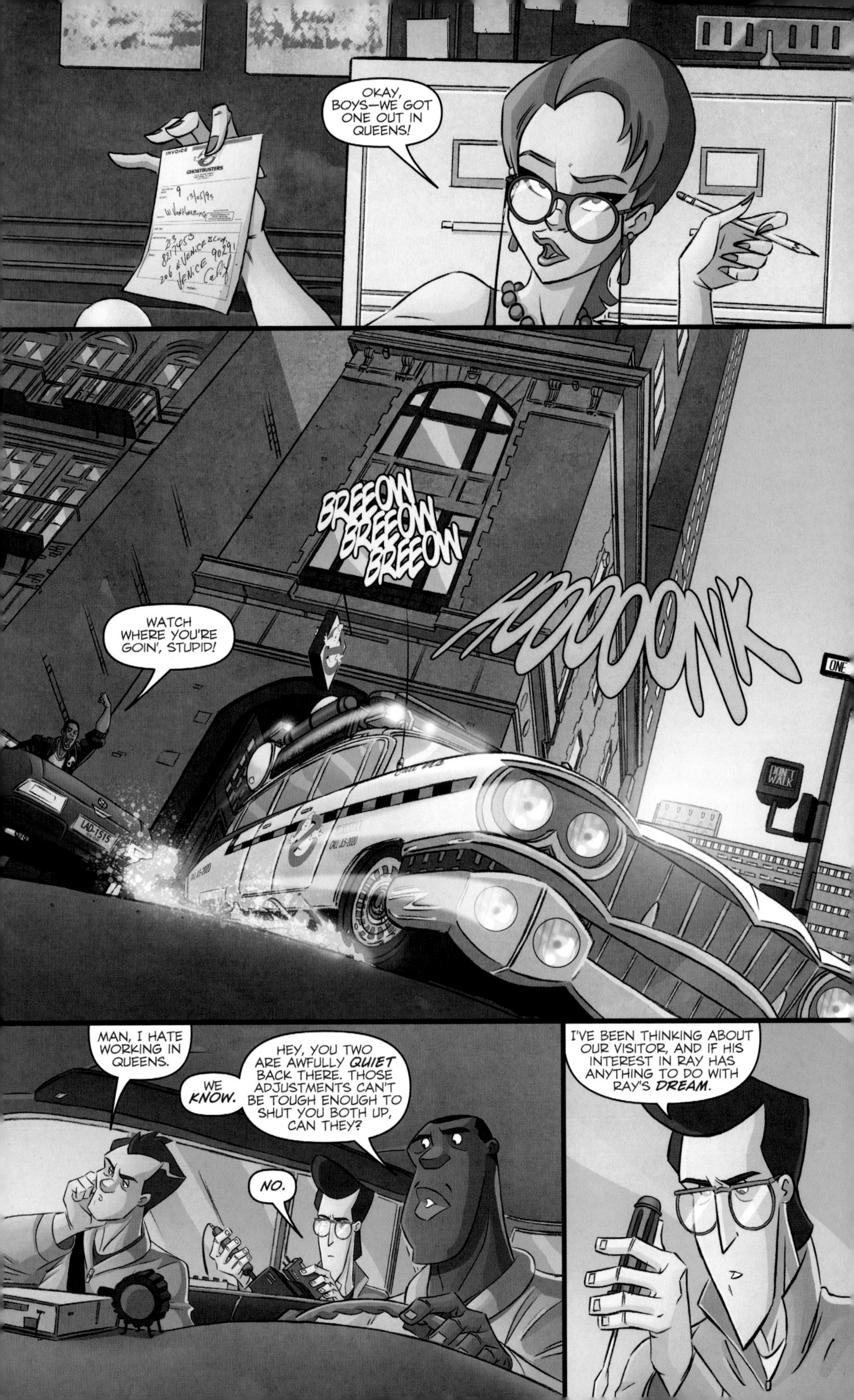
OKAY, BOYS—WE GOT ONE OUT IN QUEENS!
BREEOW BREEOW BREEOW
HOOOOONK
WATCH WHERE YOU'RE GOIN', STUPID!
ONE
DON'T WALK
MAN, I HATE WORKING IN QUEENS.
WE *KNOW*.
HEY, YOU TWO ARE AWFULLY *QUIET* BACK THERE. THOSE ADJUSTMENTS CAN'T BE TOUGH ENOUGH TO SHUT YOU BOTH UP, CAN THEY?
NO.
I'VE BEEN THINKING ABOUT OUR VISITOR, AND IF HIS INTEREST IN RAY HAS ANYTHING TO DO WITH RAY'S *DREAM*.

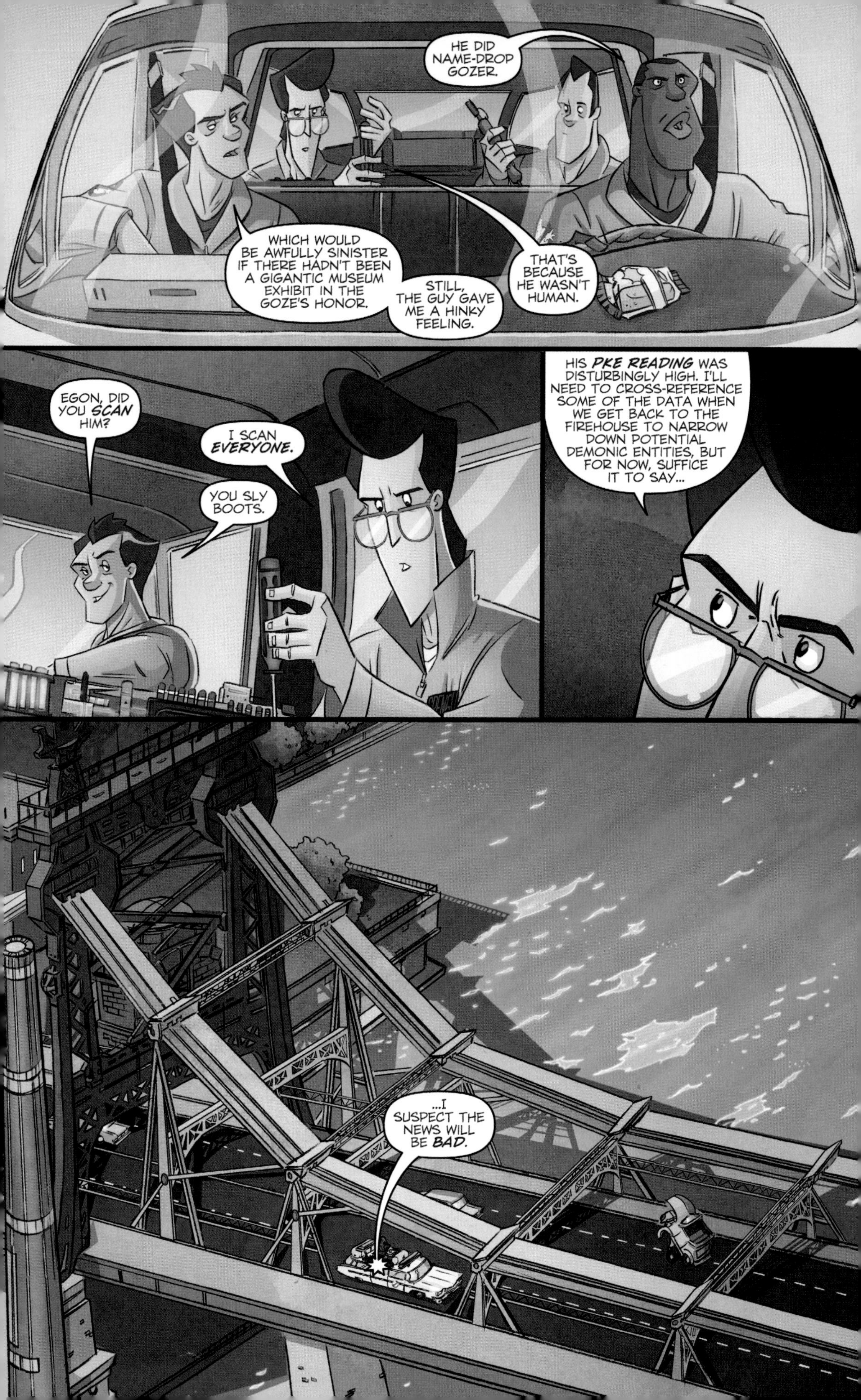
HE DID NAME-DROP GOZER.
WHICH WOULD BE AWFULLY SINISTER IF THERE HADN'T BEEN A GIGANTIC MUSEUM EXHIBIT IN THE GOZE'S HONOR.
STILL, THE GUY GAVE ME A HINKY FEELING.
THAT'S BECAUSE HE WASN'T HUMAN.
EGON, DID YOU SCAN HIM?
I SCAN EVERYONE.
YOU SLY BOOTS.
HIS PKE READING WAS DISTURBINGLY HIGH. I'LL NEED TO CROSS-REFERENCE SOME OF THE DATA WHEN WE GET BACK TO THE FIREHOUSE TO NARROW DOWN POTENTIAL DEMONIC ENTITIES, BUT FOR NOW, SUFFICE IT TO SAY...
...I SUSPECT THE NEWS WILL BE BAD.

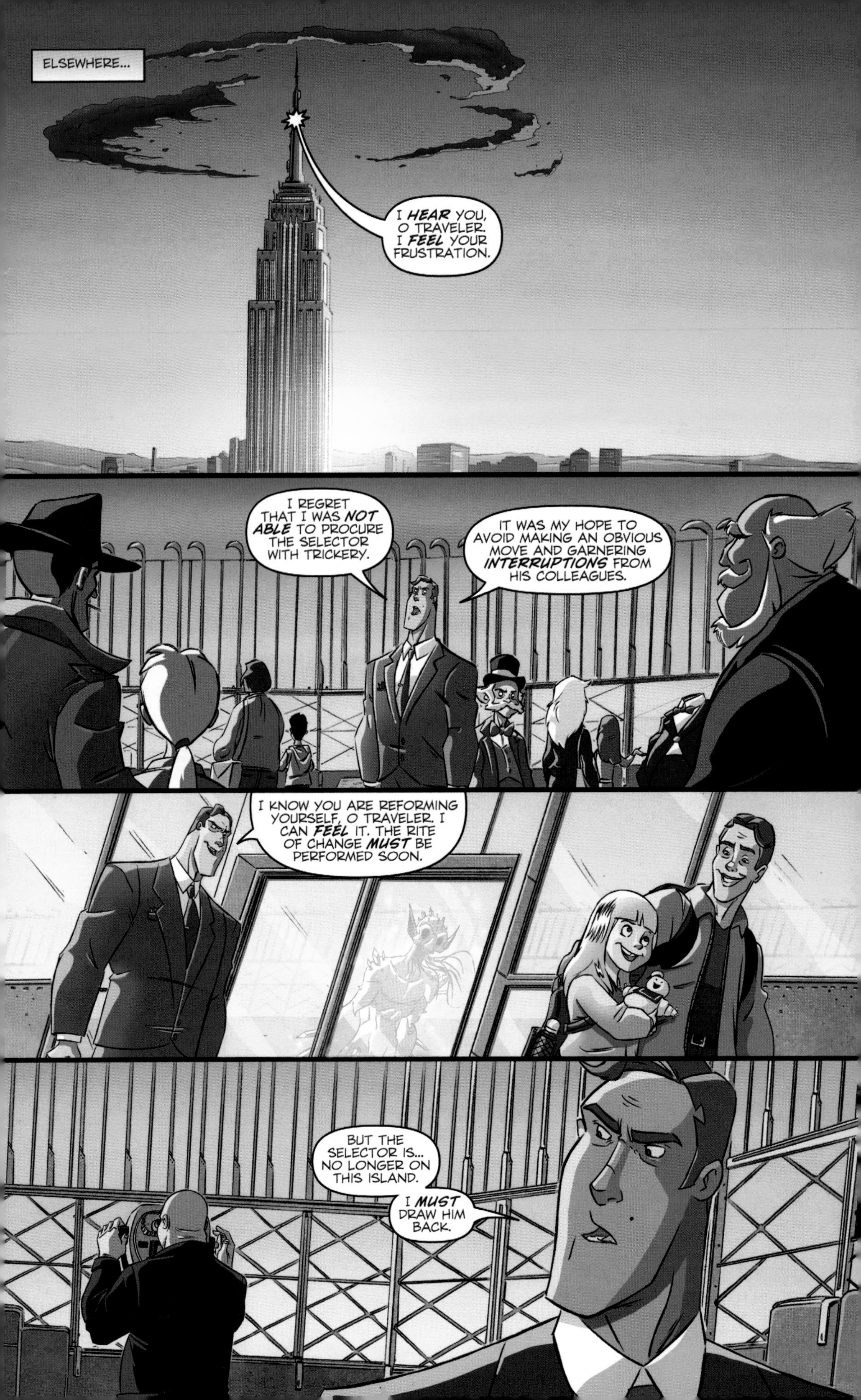
ELSEWHERE...
I HEAR YOU, O TRAVELER. I FEEL YOUR FRUSTRATION.
I REGRET THAT I WAS NOT ABLE TO PROCURE THE SELECTOR WITH TRICKERY.
IT WAS MY HOPE TO AVOID MAKING AN OBVIOUS MOVE AND GARNERING INTERRUPTIONS FROM HIS COLLEAGUES.
I KNOW YOU ARE REFORMING YOURSELF, O TRAVELER. I CAN FEEL IT. THE RITE OF CHANGE MUST BE PERFORMED SOON.
BUT THE SELECTOR IS... NO LONGER ON THIS ISLAND.
I MUST DRAW HIM BACK.

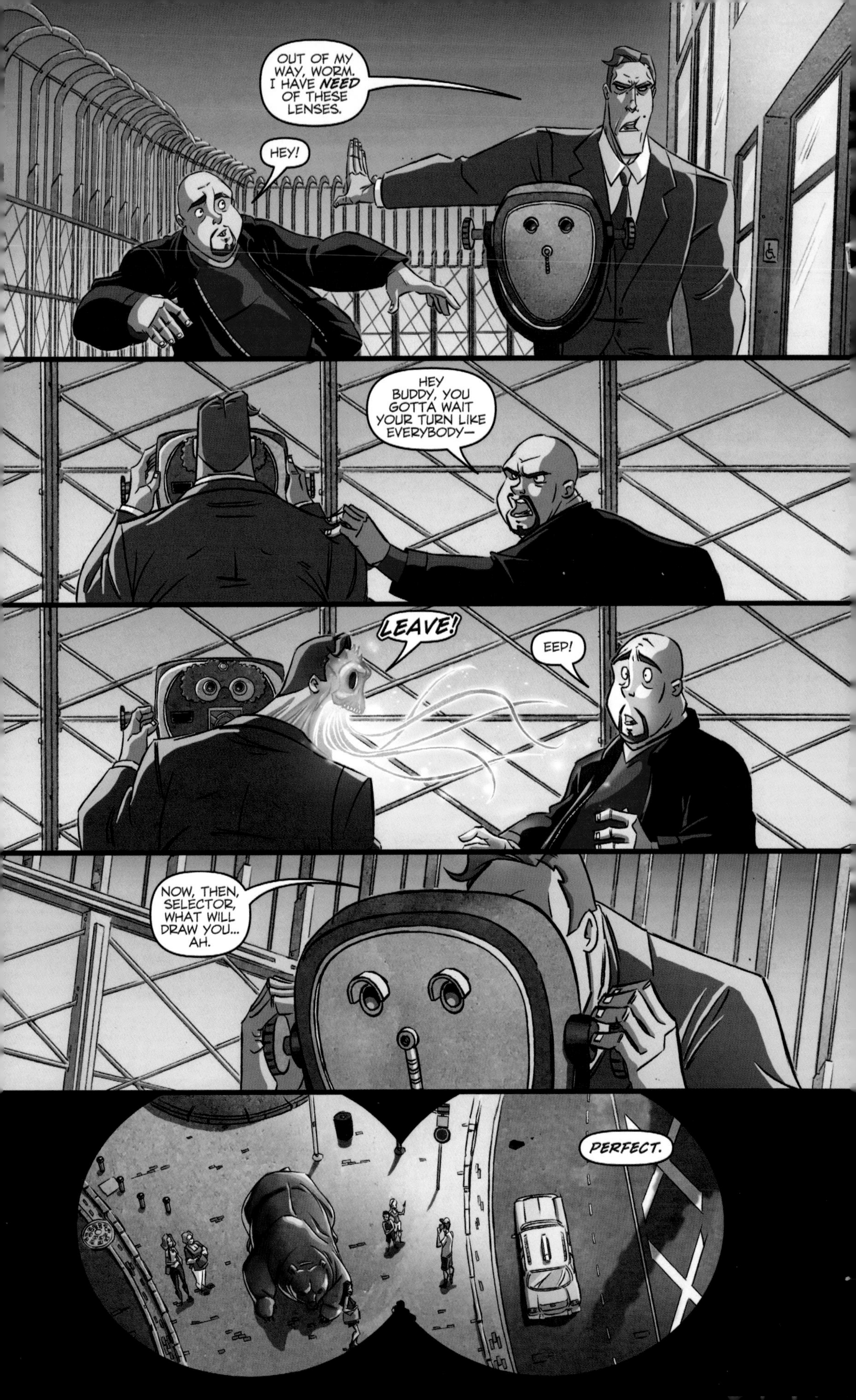
OUT OF MY WAY, WORM. I HAVE NEED OF THESE LENSES.
HEY!
HEY BUDDY, YOU GOTTA WAIT YOUR TURN LIKE EVERYBODY—
LEAVE!
EEP!
NOW, THEN, SELECTOR, WHAT WILL DRAW YOU... AH.
PERFECT.

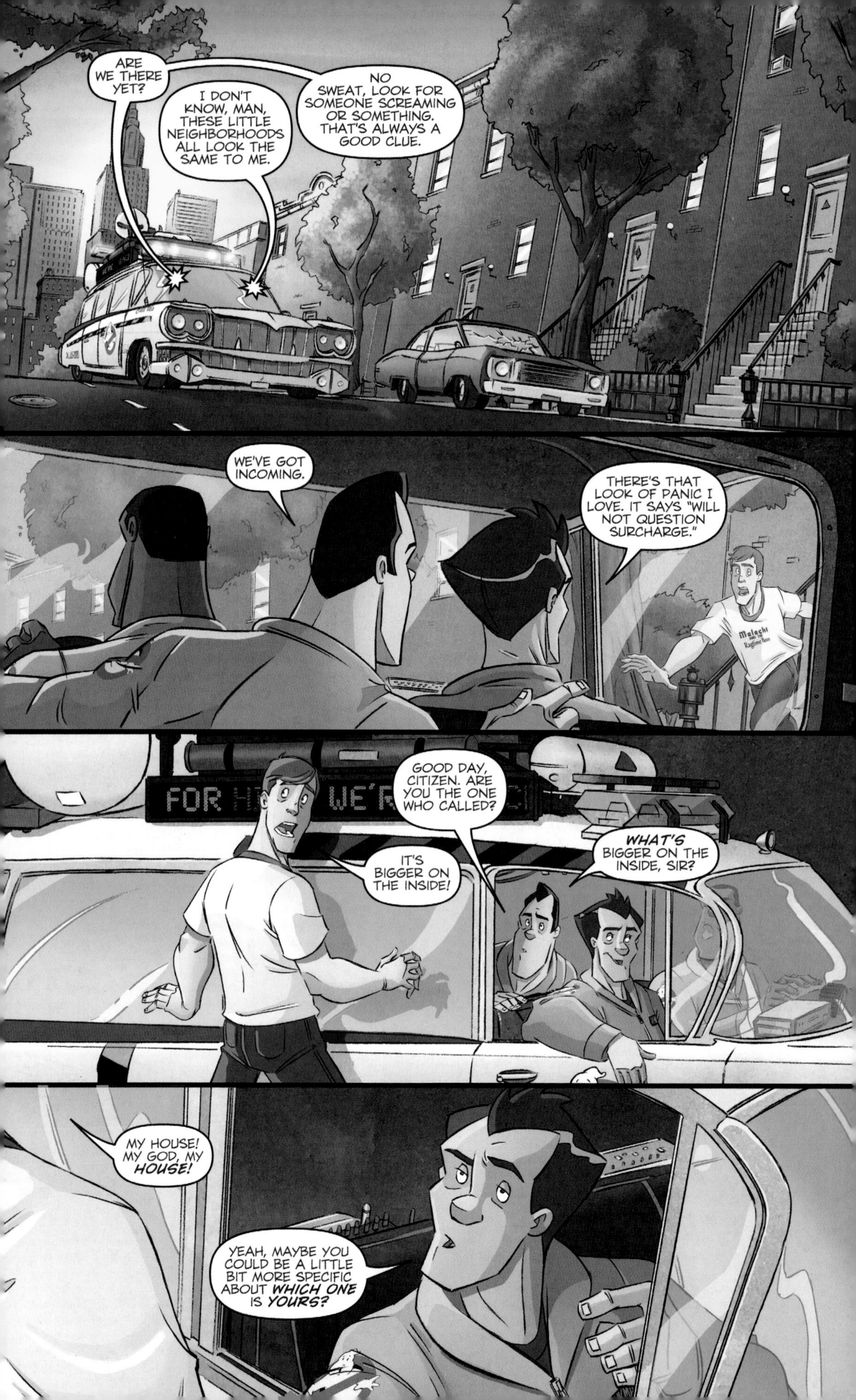
ARE WE THERE YET?
I DON'T KNOW, MAN, THESE LITTLE NEIGHBORHOODS ALL LOOK THE SAME TO ME.
NO SWEAT, LOOK FOR SOMEONE SCREAMING OR SOMETHING. THAT'S ALWAYS A GOOD CLUE.
WE'VE GOT INCOMING.
THERE'S THAT LOOK OF PANIC I LOVE. IT SAYS "WILL NOT QUESTION SURCHARGE."
GOOD DAY, CITIZEN. ARE YOU THE ONE WHO CALLED?
IT'S BIGGER ON THE INSIDE!
WHAT'S BIGGER ON THE INSIDE, SIR?
MY HOUSE! MY GOD, MY *HOUSE!*
YEAH, MAYBE YOU COULD BE A LITTLE BIT MORE SPECIFIC ABOUT *WHICH ONE* IS *YOURS?*

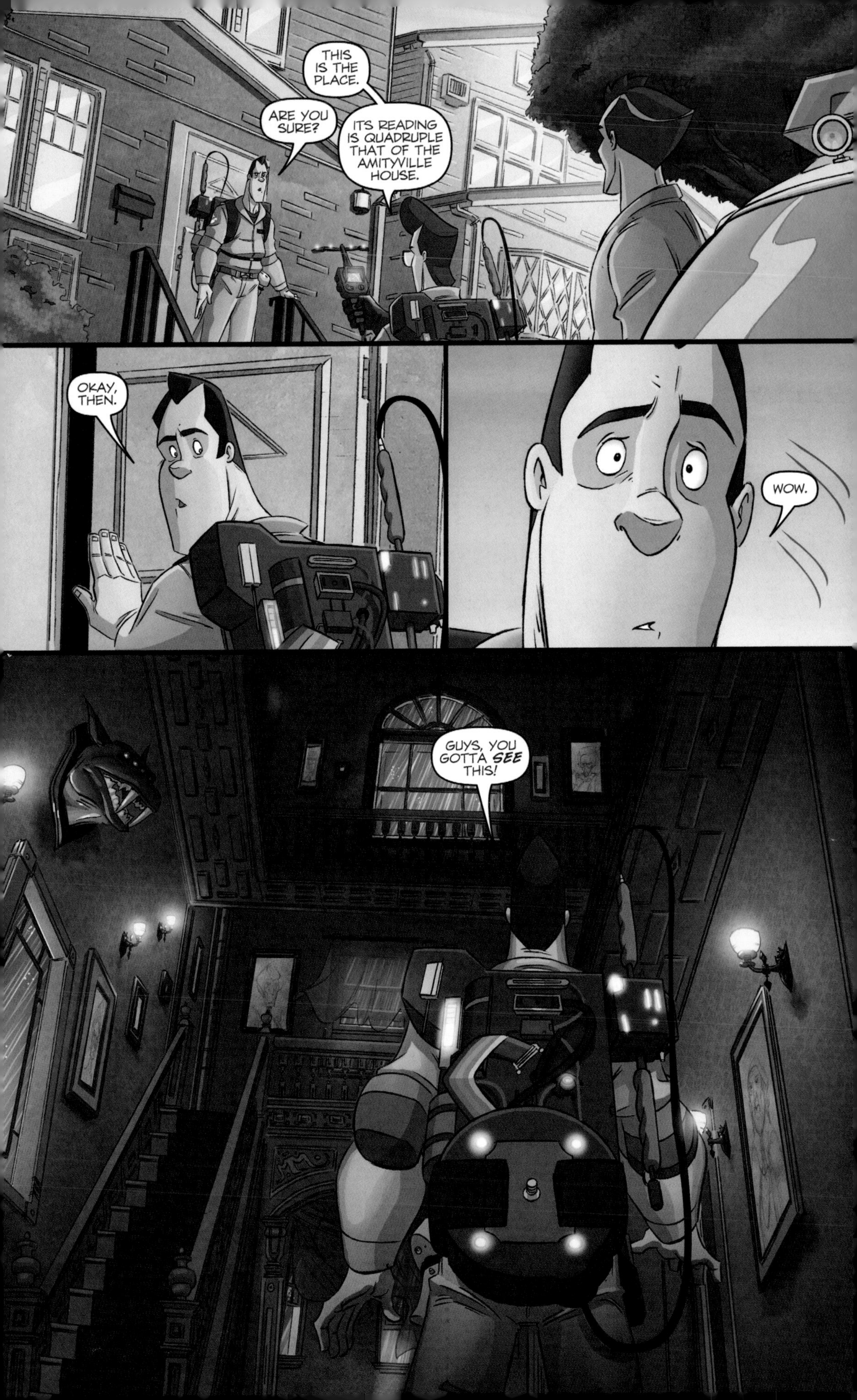
THIS IS THE PLACE.
ARE YOU SURE?
ITS READING IS QUADRUPLE THAT OF THE AMITYVILLE HOUSE.
OKAY, THEN.
WOW.
GUYS, YOU GOTTA **SEE** THIS!

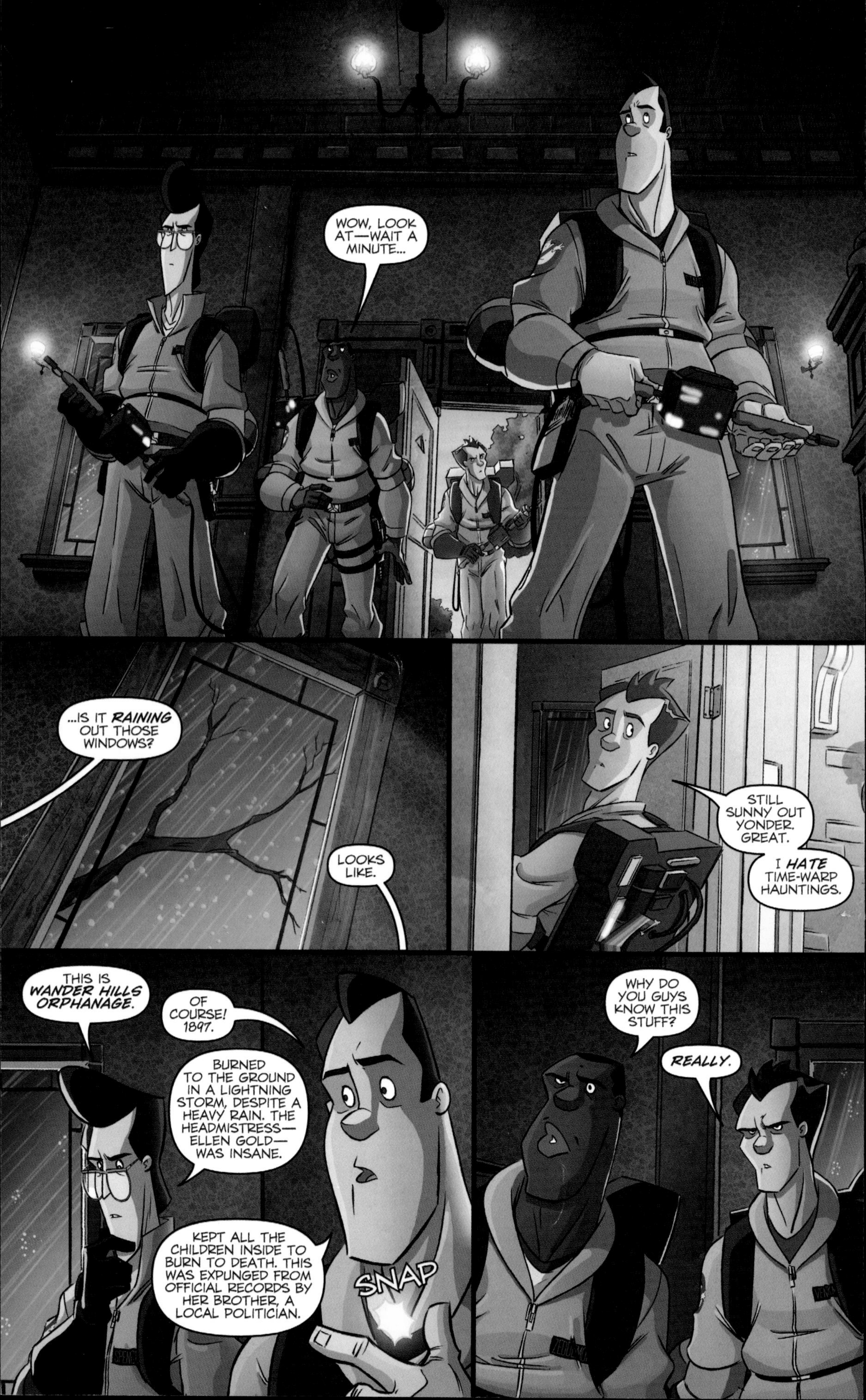
WOW, LOOK AT—WAIT A MINUTE...
...IS IT RAINING OUT THOSE WINDOWS?
LOOKS LIKE.
STILL SUNNY OUT YONDER. GREAT.
I HATE TIME-WARP HAUNTINGS.
THIS IS WANDER HILLS ORPHANAGE.
OF COURSE! 1897.
BURNED TO THE GROUND IN A LIGHTNING STORM, DESPITE A HEAVY RAIN. THE HEADMISTRESS—ELLEN GOLD—WAS INSANE.
KEPT ALL THE CHILDREN INSIDE TO BURN TO DEATH. THIS WAS EXPUNGED FROM OFFICIAL RECORDS BY HER BROTHER, A LOCAL POLITICIAN.
SNAP
WHY DO YOU GUYS KNOW THIS STUFF?
REALLY.

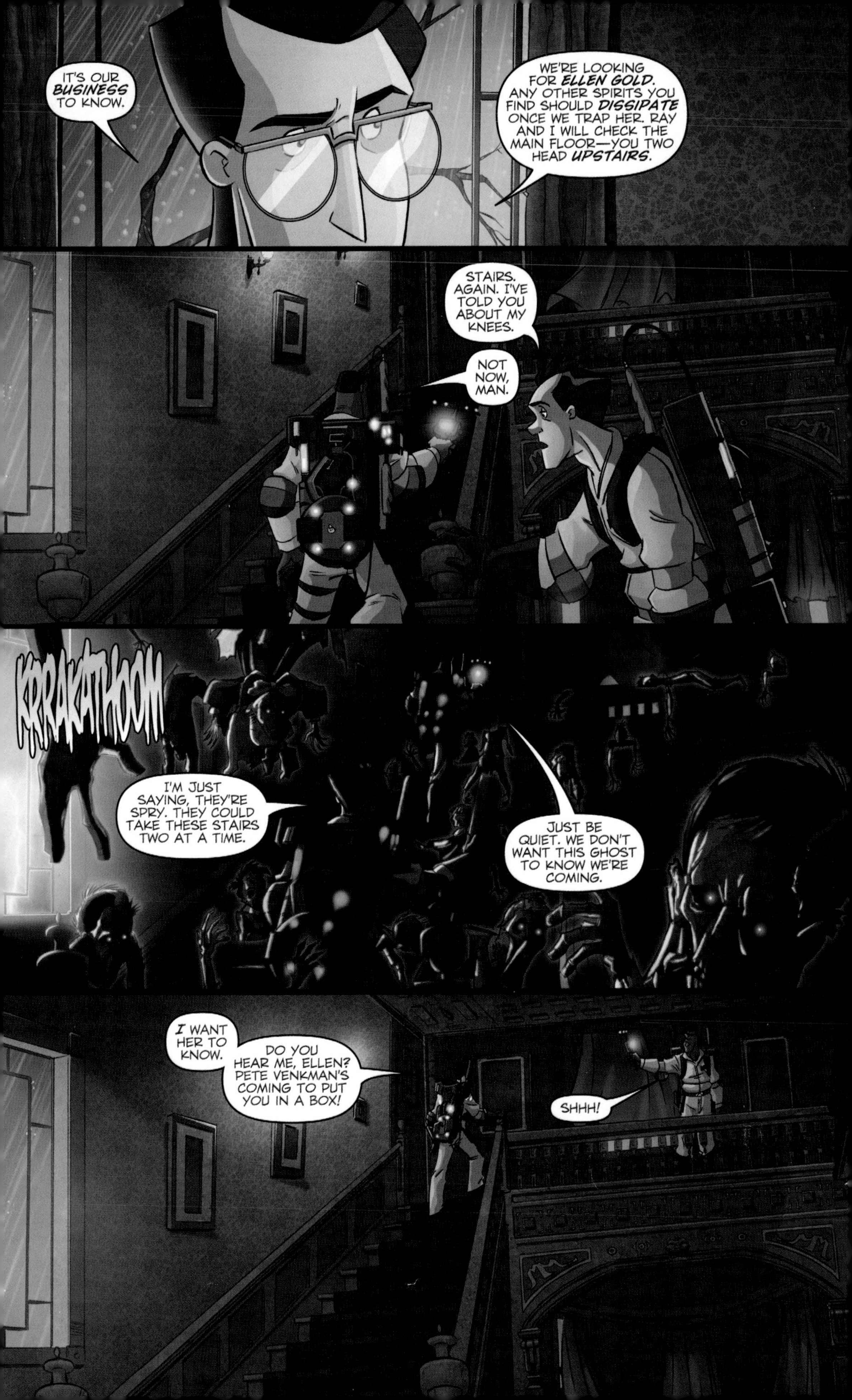
IT'S OUR BUSINESS TO KNOW.
WE'RE LOOKING FOR ELLEN GOLD. ANY OTHER SPIRITS YOU FIND SHOULD DISSIPATE ONCE WE TRAP HER. RAY AND I WILL CHECK THE MAIN FLOOR—YOU TWO HEAD UPSTAIRS.
STAIRS. AGAIN. I'VE TOLD YOU ABOUT MY KNEES.
NOT NOW, MAN.
KRRAKATHOOM
I'M JUST SAYING, THEY'RE SPRY. THEY COULD TAKE THESE STAIRS TWO AT A TIME.
JUST BE QUIET. WE DON'T WANT THIS GHOST TO KNOW WE'RE COMING.
I WANT HER TO KNOW.
DO YOU HEAR ME, ELLEN? PETE VENKMAN'S COMING TO PUT YOU IN A BOX!
SHHH!

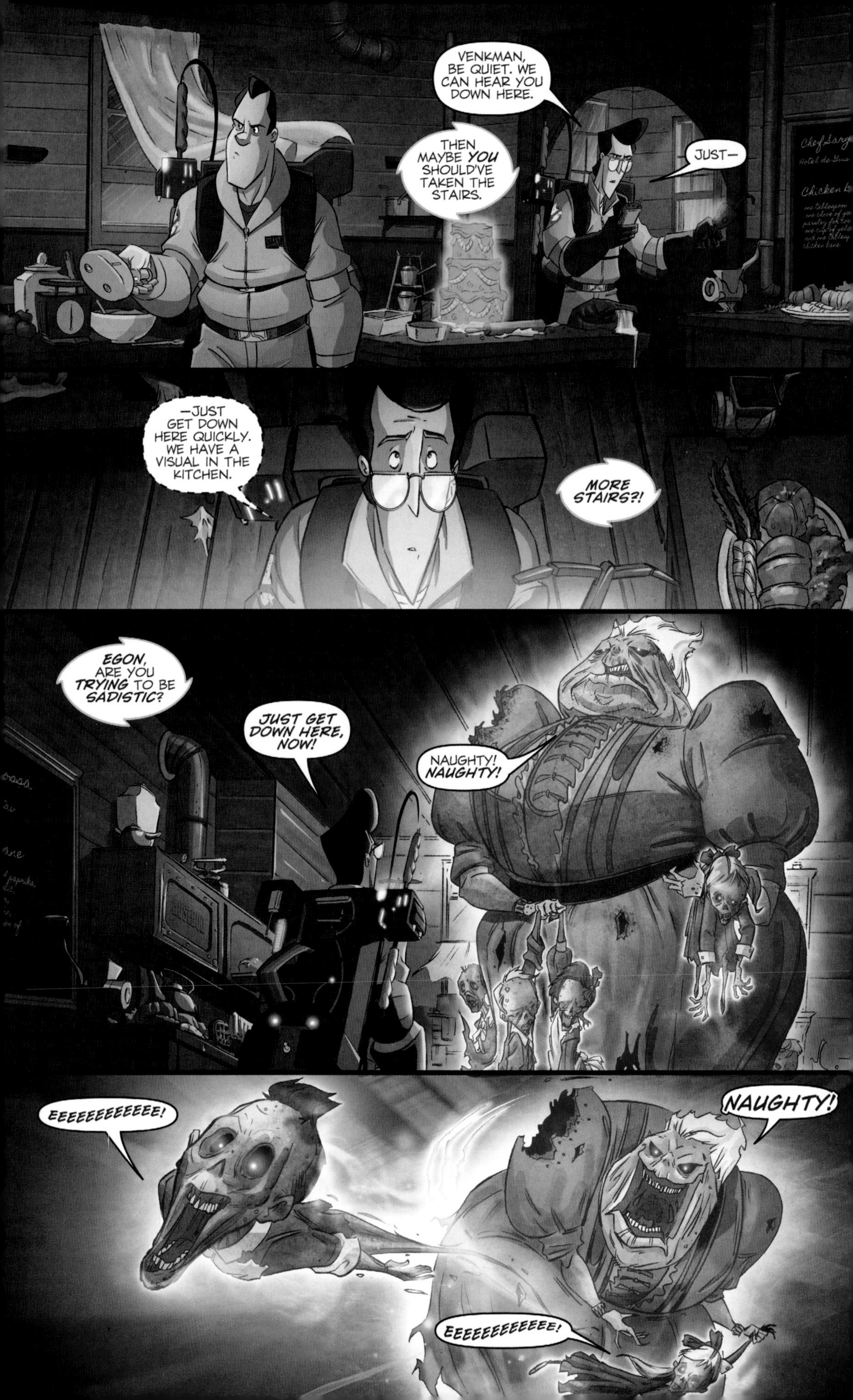

VENKMAN, BE QUIET. WE CAN HEAR YOU DOWN HERE.
THEN MAYBE YOU SHOULD'VE TAKEN THE STAIRS.
JUST—
—JUST GET DOWN HERE QUICKLY. WE HAVE A VISUAL IN THE KITCHEN.
MORE STAIRS?!
EGON, ARE YOU TRYING TO BE SADISTIC?
JUST GET DOWN HERE, NOW!
NAUGHTY! NAUGHTY!
EEEEEEEEEEEE!
NAUGHTY!
EEEEEEEEEEEE!

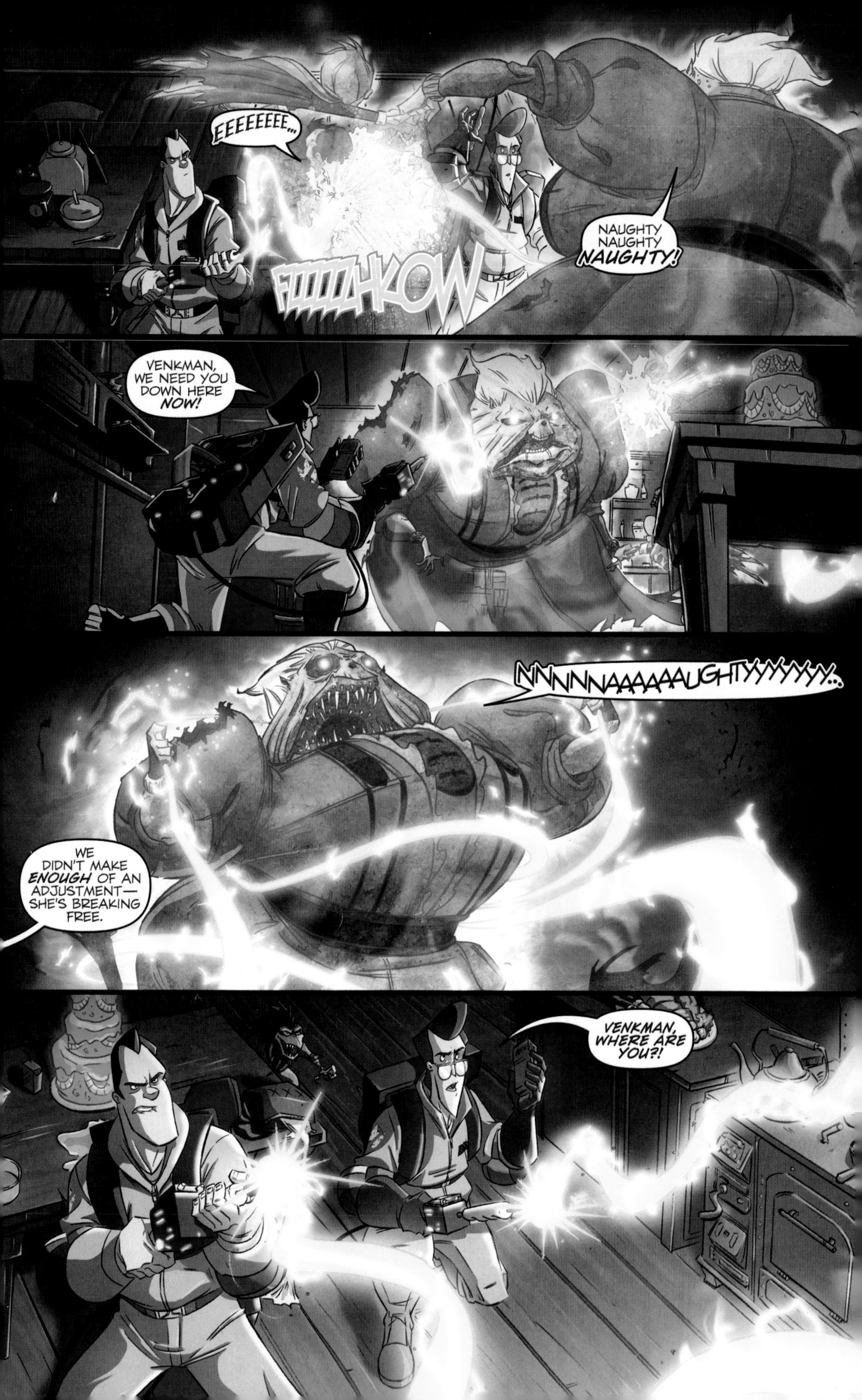
EEEEEEEE...
NAUGHTY NAUGHTY NAUGHTY!
FZZZZHKOW
VENKMAN, WE NEED YOU DOWN HERE NOW!
NNNNNAAAAAAUGHTYYYYYYY...
WE DIDN'T MAKE ENOUGH OF AN ADJUSTMENT— SHE'S BREAKING FREE.
VENKMAN, WHERE ARE YOU?!

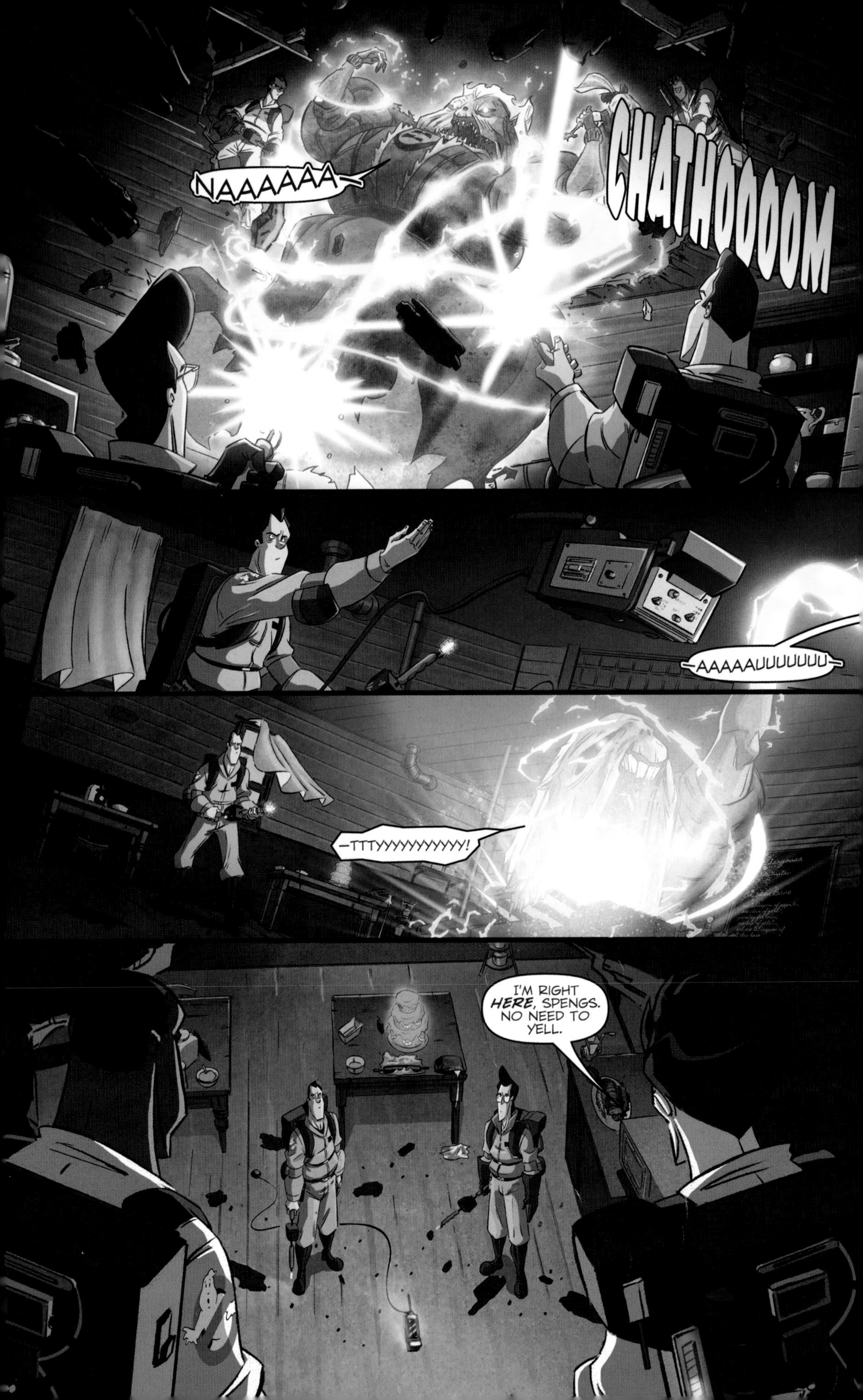
NAAAAAA—
CHATHOOOOM
—AAAAAUUUUUUU
—TTTYYYYYYYYYYYY!
I'M RIGHT *HERE*, SPENGS. NO NEED TO YELL.

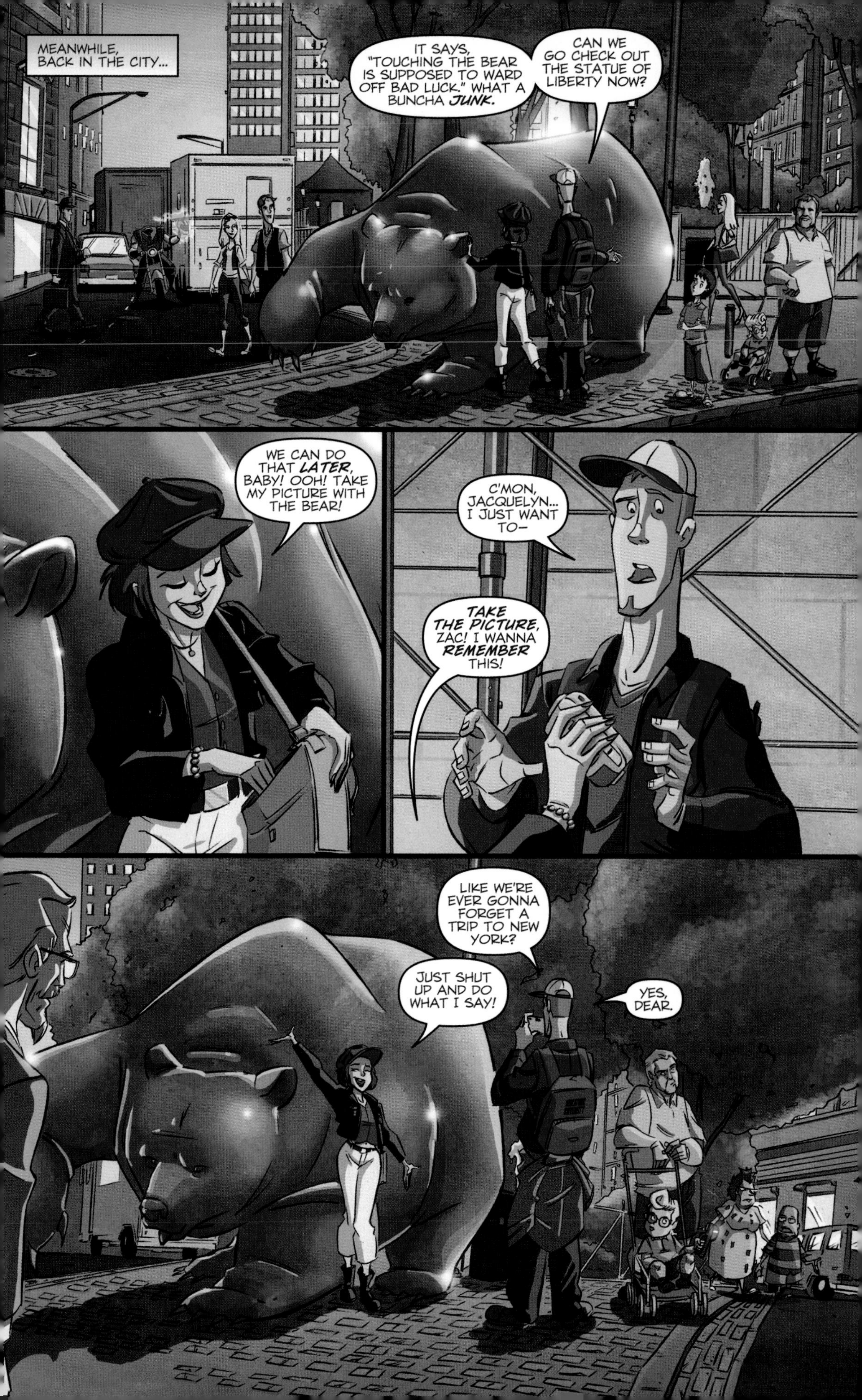
MEANWHILE, BACK IN THE CITY...
IT SAYS, "TOUCHING THE BEAR IS SUPPOSED TO WARD OFF BAD LUCK." WHAT A BUNCHA JUNK.
CAN WE GO CHECK OUT THE STATUE OF LIBERTY NOW?
WE CAN DO THAT LATER, BABY! OOH! TAKE MY PICTURE WITH THE BEAR!
C'MON, JACQUELYN... I JUST WANT TO–
TAKE THE PICTURE, ZAC! I WANNA REMEMBER THIS!
LIKE WE'RE EVER GONNA FORGET A TRIP TO NEW YORK?
JUST SHUT UP AND DO WHAT I SAY!
YES, DEAR.

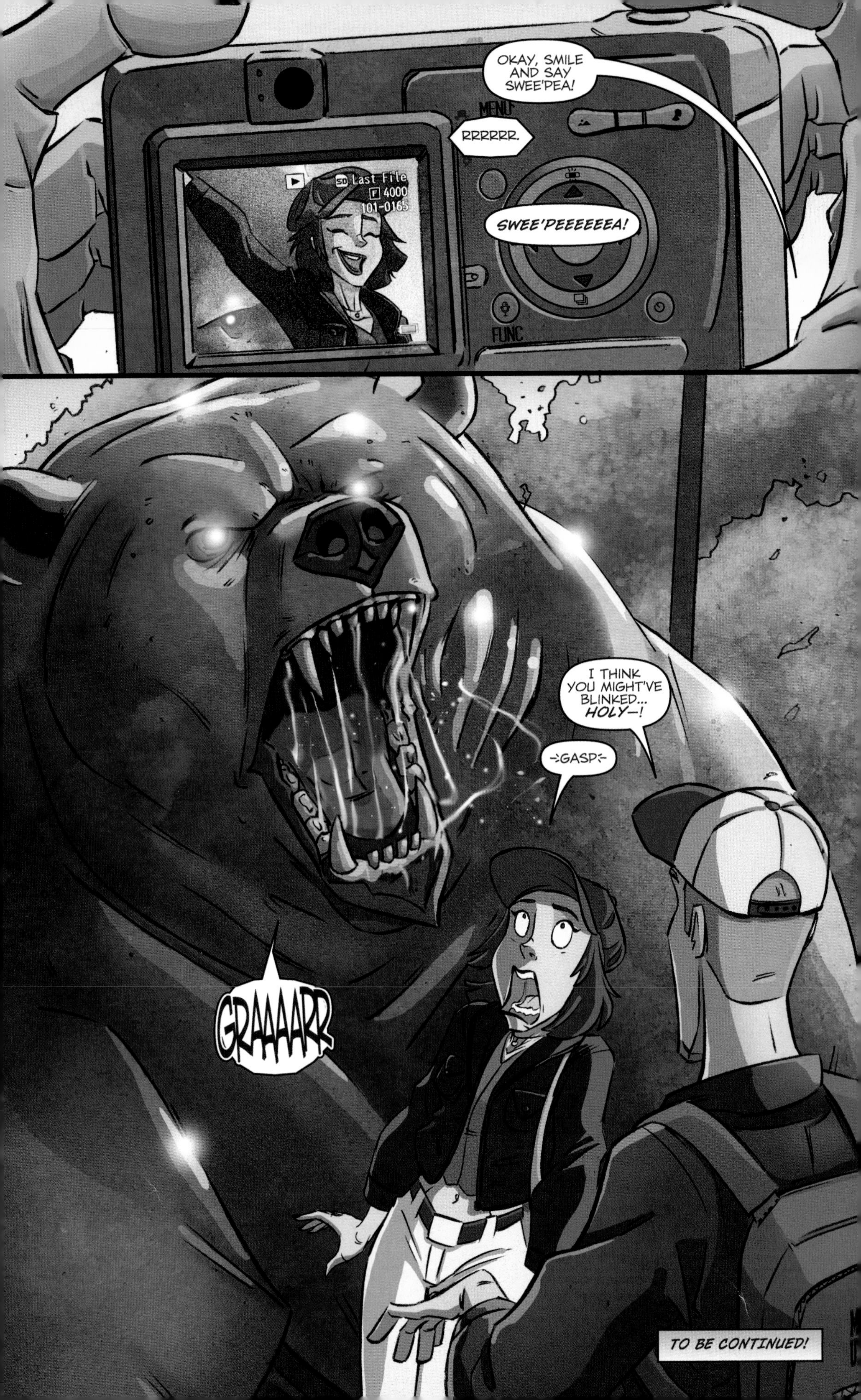
OKAY, SMILE AND SAY SWEE'PEA!
RRRRRR.
Last File
4000
101-0165
SWEE'PEEEEEEA!
MENU
FUNC
I THINK YOU MIGHT'VE BLINKED... HOLY—!
GASP
GRAAAARR
TO BE CONTINUED!

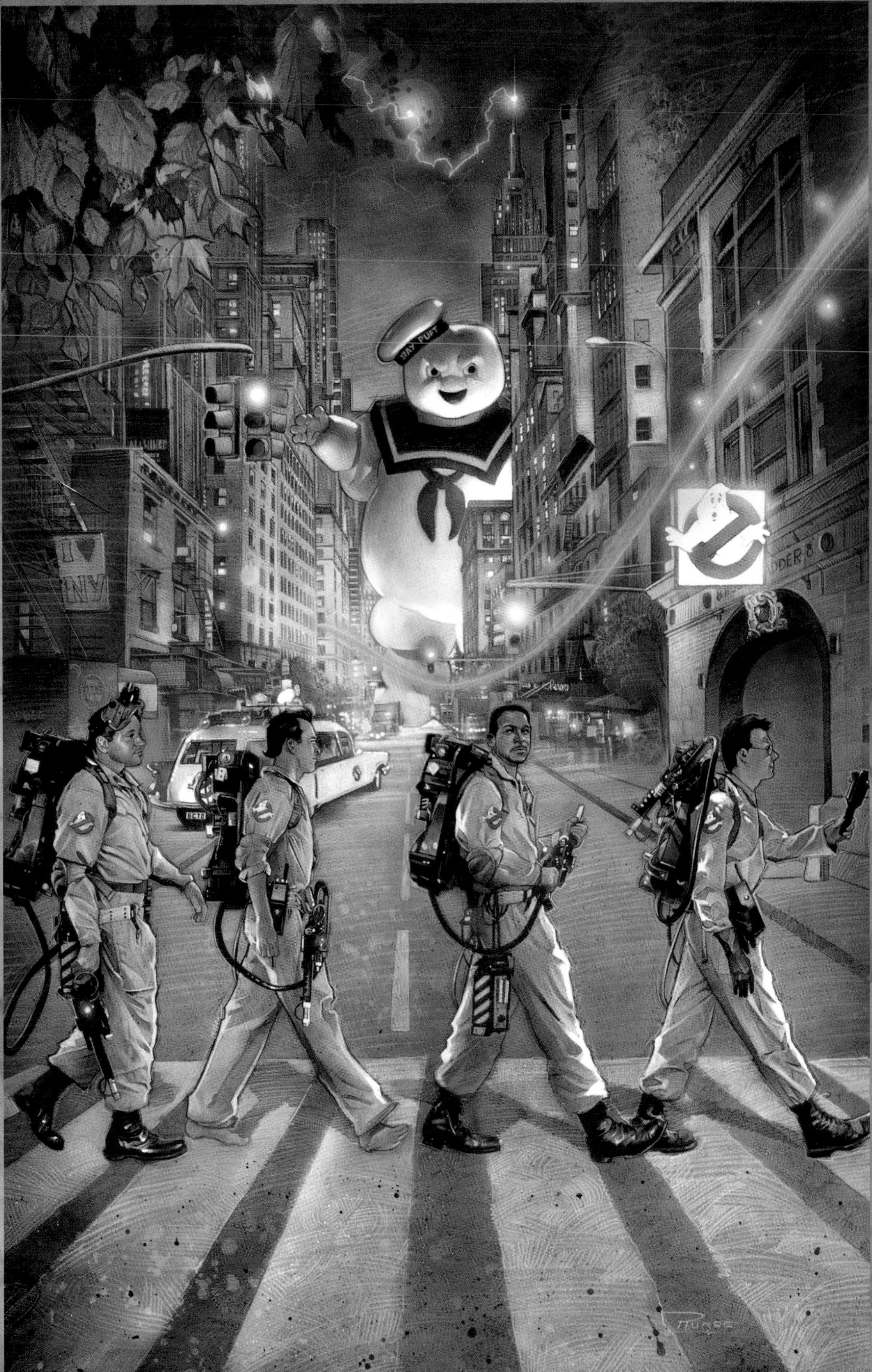
STAY PUFT
I ♥ NY
LADDER 8
ECTO
RUNGE

GHOSTBUSTERS ISSUE #2, COVER B
ART BY NICK RUNGE

GHOSTBUSTERS™

COLLECT THEM ALL!

Set of 12 Hardcover Books ISBN: 978-1-61479-484-4

Volume One: The Man from the Mirror, Parts 1–4

Hardcover Book ISBN	Hardcover Book ISBN	Hardcover Book ISBN	Hardcover Book ISBN
978-1-61479-485-1	978-1-61479-486-8	978-1-61479-487-5	978-1-61479-488-2

Volume Two: The Most Magical Place on Earth, Parts 1–4

Hardcover Book ISBN	Hardcover Book ISBN	Hardcover Book ISBN	Hardcover Book ISBN
978-1-61479-489-9	978-1-61479-490-5	978-1-61479-491-2	978-1-61479-492-9

Volume Three: Haunted America, Parts 1–4

Hardcover Book ISBN	Hardcover Book ISBN	Hardcover Book ISBN	Hardcover Book ISBN
978-1-61479-493-6	978-1-61479-494-3	978-1-61479-495-0	978-1-61479-496-7